A Treasure Trove of Tales

© Copyright, 2024, Tanmayishri Sumanth—Author & Illustrator

All rights reserved. No part of this book may be reproduced, stored in a retrieval system, or transmitted, in any form by any means, electronic, mechanical, magnetic, optical, chemical, manual, photocopying, recording or otherwise, without the prior written consent of its writer.

First Edition, 2024

ISBN: 978-93-5621-615-0

A TREASURE TROVE OF TALES

WRITTEN AND ILLUSTRATED BY
TANMAYISHRI SUMANTH

OrangeBooks Publication
www.orangebooks.in

OrangeBooks Publication

"A TREASURE TROVE OF TALES" is the first work of fiction, authored and illustrated by Tanmayishri Sumanth, a vibrant fifth grader from Chennai. She had a flair for the English language and read independently by age five. This voracious reader loves the company of books, and her creative pursuits include writing, drawing, painting and singing. She feeds her curiosity by reading new authors, discussing her readings animatedly or enacting a puppetry. She uses a narrative style of writing in her imaginative stories and poetry. Her work is sprinkled with subtle humour and evolving value systems and is both engaging and entertaining.

I Dedicate This Book

To My

Wonderful And Intelligent Brother,
Prem,

Who Brings Out The Humour In Me.

CONTENTS

Acknowledgements xi
Who Is This Book For?.............................. xiii
What Is This Book About?......................... xv

1. The Hunters and The Lion......................... 1
2. The Magic Buds.. 8
3. Dreams Come True! 14
4. The Fountain of Luck............................... 23
5. The Magic Canyon 31
6. Shoes On Strike! 37
7. The Curse of a Sage.................................. 40
8. The Prince and The Cave......................... 46
9. The Divine Power 52
10. The Ishavriksha Tribe............................... 58
11. The Brave King.. 65
12. Deep In the Jungle 70
13. The Watermelon Tree............................... 74
14. The Animals and The Monster.............. 80
15. Aha, Oho and Hehe 85
16. The Clever Minister.................................. 92
17. The Flying Veena..................................... 100

18. On The Night Of Halloween 105
19. The Pumpkin Juice Mystery 108
20. The Appliance Store Adventure 114
21. The Magic Book 118
22. The Big Problem 125
23. My Dream Land 130

ACKNOWLEDGEMENTS

I express immense gratitude to all the authors who wrote the many books I have read. I must make a special mention of the Harry Potter series, written by JK. Rowling. They were the ones that inspired me to write fiction!

Dear reader, I also thank you, for choosing to read this book. It really means a lot to me!

I would like to thank all the elders in my life for answering my many questions. My special thanks to my teachers for motivating and encouraging me so much.

My heartfelt thanks to the OrangeBooks Publication team for publishing my first book.

Last, but not the least, my deepest gratitude to my loving parents for being my strength and for their role in making this book a reality.

WHO IS THIS BOOK FOR?

This book is for the ages 1 to 100. If you think babies don't read, let me make myself clear that I'm referring to prodigies.

Just kidding!

Well, I'm ten years old, and I think children between 5 and 15 years of age will enjoy the contents of this book.

There is a lot of bravery, magic, adventure and a bit of humour within these pages.

So be valiant, wear your armour and gallop away in your white horse, straight into this book.

If you don't have an armour or a white horse, use your strength and courage to lift a finger and flip the page.

Happy reading!!!

WHAT IS THIS BOOK ABOUT?

Do you know what awaits you,

If you turn a page?

Is it a monster, maybe a few,

Or a king, or a sage?

Could there be a trickster,

Plotting something sinister?

Almost all the stories in this book,

I bring to your attention!

(If you don't believe me, you can look)

Are actually plain fiction!

THE HUNTERS AND THE LION

[This Story Is Dedicated To One Of My Favourite Authors, Roddy Doyle.]

Dear reader,

Every book needs some humour, so I added some in this one, too.

I hope I didn't add too much, because then the book wouldn't be stacked among the books in school libraries.

Do read on!

"Hans? Can we have a snack?"

"No, Doris! We just had two biscuits!"

"Quiet, both of you! I think a deer is coming."

In the heart of a dense jungle, on a large, hollow tree with thick branches, were three hunters. Doris, a short, fat man with blond hair and a rather high-pitched voice. He was a foodie and loved meat. Hans, who was Doris' brother, was a thin, fair man with dark hair and a quiet voice, and their leader Jones was a tall, burly, strict man with a black moustache.

The trio sat uncomfortably on the large, wide branches of the tree, looking down, tensed, waiting for an animal to get caught in the net below, which they had laid earlier. They had sat there for more than an hour or two, when—

"Rrrr… Grrrr… Drrrr…"

"Jones! I heard something!"

"Oh, Hans! Please, would you stop making so much noi—

Wait, what did you say?"

"I heard a growling noise!"

Oooh, a lion! It would sell at the market for more than ten gold coins! We will be so rich!"

"Erm… Jones?

I don't think it was a lion…

It was my stomach rumbling…

Sorry, boss."

"OH! Doris! For heavens' sake, stop it! Hans, give him some bread.

"On it, boss."

Doris devoured the bread greedily, as he thought, "Poor me! I am being fed so very little! I want to go to the butcher shop! There, I can buy so much meat!"

Meanwhile, at the butcher shop —

"AAAAGGGGHHHHH!

A lion!!! Help, Help!

Somebody…ANYBODY!!!"

Doris was lucky he was not at the butcher shop! After few moments, the lion ate all the meat and went to the zoo.

At the zoo—

"Help!

A LION HAS ESCAPED!

Someone HELP!"

All the tourists ran away. The lion tried to bite a tourist but luckily, the tourist escaped, unharmed.

(If you want to know some details, the lion bit into a piece of cloth the tourist wore. For more details, the lion was left holding between his teeth, a torn pair of trousers and a tiny bit of something MORE. Make of that what you will.)

The lion travelled to many places, and created chaos, screams and shouts, wherever he went.

In the meantime, at the forest—

"Boss, let's go home. I don't think we'll catch any animal today."

"Doris, be quiet. Listen, I'll make a deal. If we go without catching an animal, I'll give you three hamburgers."

Doris gladly agreed to Jones.

Meanwhile, when the lion was done scaring everyone, he went straight back to the jungle.

And guess what? He went exactly where our hunters' net was, and Jones, who was alert, pulled the ropes and trapped the lion quickly. The three happy men went straight to the market with the frustrated lion, and sold it to a rich merchant.

Everything was back to normal, and everyone got what they wanted (except Doris, who had looked forward to the three hamburgers, and the lion, who hadn't wanted to be caught after enjoying himself so much. "That bite felt really good. I'll come back for MORE.", thought the trapped lion.).

The three men divided the money among themselves, the butcher stacked his shop with fresh, tasty meat, the zoo ensured that cages were locked safely, and the tourist who got his trousers (AND what was underneath it) bit off, bought a pair of new ones for a very cheap price!

By the way, if you cannot guess what 'MORE' means in the story, it's underwear. Poor tourist.

If you tour around the world anytime, be careful about what's behind you.

It could just be this lion— that merchant had to buy a LOT more 'MORE' than you could imagine.

BEWARE— It could be you next!

THE TOURIST RUNNING AWAY AS THE LION BIT OFF... HEHEHE!

THE MAGIC BUDS

In a small village in Asia, there was a small, straw hut. It had been there for more than a decade, and was the home of a girl named Akshara, a 11-year-old who lived with her mother.

Akshara was a rather simple looking girl, with green eyes and a quaint little face. They were very poor, and could hardly afford two meals in a day. Her mother worked as a maid servant for a rich merchant in the village, and with the little money she earned, she would try to make both the ends meet.

One day, the merchant announced his decision to move to another village to make profit in his business. That meant Akshara's mother couldn't work for the merchant to earn the day's wages! What would they do for their food? She asked all the villagers if they needed a servant. But none of them required her services.

It was one of those difficult times. Akshara had to go for a whole day without meals! When it was time to sleep, she went to her mat, sad and hungry. She started crying silently.

Suddenly, POOF! An angel appeared, holding three buds. She said, "I know you suffer, my child, and that is why I am here. Take these buds. These flower buds will help you in times of need. Remember, you can use each of these buds only once. Use them wisely. Chant this prayer to open them.

'Magic bud, heed my call.

Please help me, once and for all.'

The buds will close themselves, and disappear, after satisfying your request. God bless you, child." Saying these words, the angel disappeared.

Akshara looked at the three buds placed in front of her, and whispered the prayer,

"Magic bud, heed my call.

Please help me, once and for all."

At once, one of the buds blossomed into a beautiful flower. It radiated a bright and happy light. Akshara's hunger faded away, and she felt comfortable. She lay down on her mat, and slept peacefully, with a content smile on her face.

The next morning, her mother exclaimed, "Yesterday night, I had a really peaceful sleep! It was an amazing night! Also, I have good news to share with you, dear! Our neighbour Teja needs some help washing the dishes, and she has come up with a good offer with a rather high price. I have agreed. Life is getting better!"

Akshara couldn't agree more. She remembered what happened last night. The magic buds did work. One of the buds that removed her hunger and plight had disappeared last night, after she slept. She had placed the other two buds safely in her cupboard.

Next, she decided to get some fresh air by going for a walk. She took the remaining two buds with her. Suddenly, she heard a voice screaming, "Please help me, a lion is chasing me! HELP!" A lion had wandered out of the forest!

Akshara did not have any knife or a sharp object near her, but decided to help the villager with her buds. She chanted the magic words, and the bud turned into a flower, and expanded in size! It was as large as an elephant! Then Akshara heard a clanking noise. Seven knights in steel armour ran out of the stem of the flower, and killed the lion. POOF! The knights and the flower vanished.

It was getting late, and Akshara went back home. Her mother earned a lot of money from her work and bought a lot of food and other comforts for their home. She thought of the times when she was poor, and had to go for a day without food.

So, Akshara decided to use the third and last bud to provide food and shelter for poor children. She chanted,

"Magic bud, heed my call.
Please help me once and for all."

And out of the third bud flashed a bright, white light, next to her house appeared a large mansion. Inside it, there were many shelves stacked with books, toys, food, board games and many other fun things! And the mansion served the poor children for many generations!

A Treasure Trove of Tales

MAGIC BUDS

DREAMS COME TRUE!

Hello, dear readers!

Have you ever had a realistic dream?

Well, I have. And when I have such a dream, I wake up and ponder whether it could become real.

Ever heard of the idiom, "Dreams come true"?

Here's a story of a girl who really did have one!

Have fun reading!

In a small town there lived a dreamy and cute girl named Aria. Her mother, a dentist, practiced at her own clinic. Her father, a mechanic, worked at a nearby garage that he owned.

Aria was always having very queer dreams. When she narrated them to her busy mother, she got the reply— "Be quiet and find something to work on!" Her father just laughed and told her not to believe such silly things. So, she wrote them in her rough notebook.

One of her dreams was very funny and silly, and it actually became real! Aria's name in the dream was Eve. She lived in a place surrounded by many mountains and trees. There were five monsters, too. Their names were Chesty, Sandy, Woody, Misty and Webby.

Eve was a very wise, clever and intelligent girl in the village where she lived. She solved and had answers to all the problems, queries, disputes and quarrels of the villagers.

One cloudy day, the five monsters wanted to know who among them was the best poet. To gain clarity on this, they went to Eve's house. Eve knew it to be a difficult question, because the monsters were all fine poets.

Eve gave them a week to come up with a poem and it should be related to the topic: My home is the best home. All the monsters agreed. Only Sandy seemed a bit nervous; so, Eve teamed her up with Chesty.

The monsters went home to complete the task they were given, their thoughts focused on writing a good poem, with creative quotes and lines.

One week flew past, and it was time to present each of their work. They walked towards Eve's house, chatting away about their poems exuberantly. They were excited to show their poems to Eve.

Sandy and Chesty were the first in line. Excitedly, both of them recited in unison…

"The deserted land we dwell in,

The rocky, sandy cavern,

Full of pure nothingness

Silence is easy to earn,

Full of cactus, date palm and more
But even then,
Chestnuts are what we yearn."

Then Webby piped up:
"Oh, I make my point clear,
That my home, strong and tough,
Is made of plain leaves and twigs,
I'll give an explanation, rough,
The roof is made of daffodils,
And the doors of dandelions,
The walls made of water lilies
And structure, made by creative minds!"

Next, Woody sang,
"The place I live in,
Is dark, dusty, and perfect for me!
I describe it thus, as the best home,
It is firm and woody

And definitely suits me!"

Lastly, Misty recited,

"My place is full of
Leaves, plants and beasts,
And my lovely home is covered with,
Soft bushes and trees."

"Bravo! Excellent work, all of you. I have now decided the best poet among the five of you. All of you clap hands for Woody!", declared Eve.

She saw the monsters' confused looks. She explained her decision to choose Woody as the best poet. Eve said, "I chose him because he was the only one who told the truth. He also gave reasons as to why he liked his home."

Eve continued her explanation, "Chesty and Sandy, you mentioned in your poem the you still yearn for chestnuts, and it sounded like you were not contented with your place.

Misty just described how his home looks like. Webby's poem is full of fantasy and creativity, but not about his real home.

Remember the title I gave you all was 'My home is the best home.' I gave the title on purpose to see what you all would write about. Actually, there is no such thing as the 'best home.' Every home is a good home as long as you feel happy, staying there.

You sang about what kind of homes you like. We all understand that not everyone has the same preference. You forgot to mention in your poem that it is YOU who likes your home.

Woody added these two specific lines in his small poem, *'It definitely suits me' and '... it is perfect for me'*, which is why I chose him."

"Great job, all of you!", praised Eve, "I admit I am impressed by your talent; so, I hereby make an announcement: That you all are now the *'Village writers'* and you are assigned to write notes of all the important occurrences in the village."

All the monsters were overjoyed with the job given to them. The people of the village applauded Eve; she was named '*The Solver of Problems*' and was presented with a ukulele, the traditional instrument of that village, as a gift.

Of course, this was all just a dream, and Aria woke up, when she felt something hard under her head. When she checked under her pillow,

SURPRISE!

Strange but true, there lay a sparkling ukulele, shining brightly at her!

This was a miracle!

She tried to play the ukulele, which she had never learned to play before.

She pulled the strings, and out came a melodious, lyrical tune!

It was a magic instrument.

Her parents couldn't believe it, either!

The ukulele from Aria's dream became a reality!

Dear readers, make sure to believe in your dreams too, like Aria. Because dreams DO come true!

Goodnight and sweet dreams!

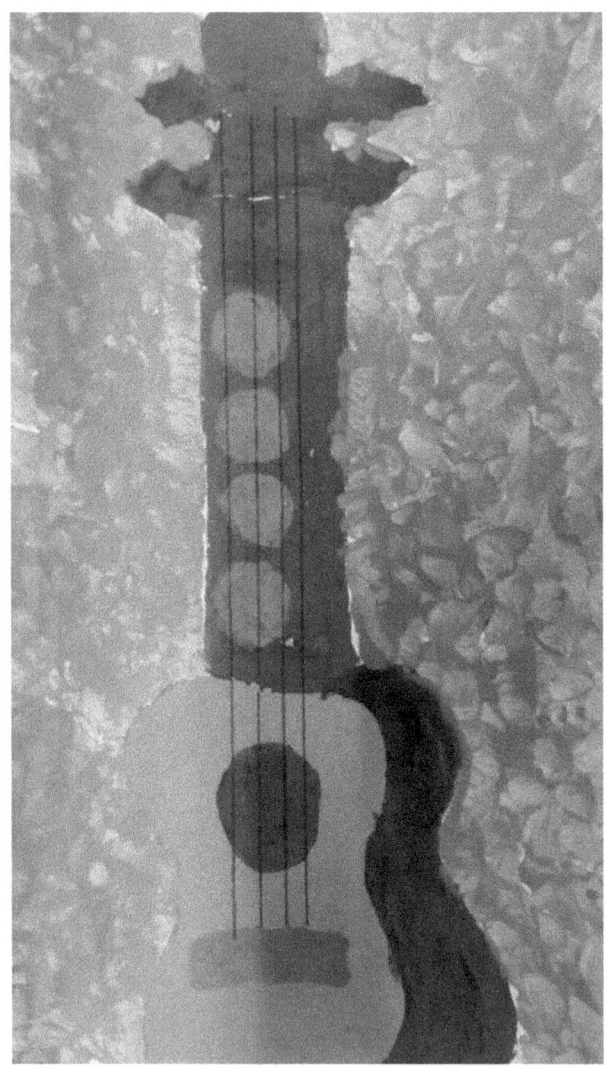

THE MAGICAL UKULELE

THE FOUNTAIN OF LUCK

In a valley, deep in a forest, there was a magic fountain. Anyone who bathed in it, be it animal or human, would be granted their heart's deepest desire. The only entrance to the forest was through the Jinteroo Village.

The lucky soul, who gets chosen to go to the fountain, would have an almost perfect life; filled with peace and calm.

Yes, they had to be chosen by a SPECIAL BEING! An oracle of the goddess would appear with a stick and tap the Lucky One on the head. No one was chosen randomly as the Lucky One.

The oracle would choose only the most kind and innocent person in the village. The people of the village concluded that if the oracle didn't appear, the year was not auspicious.

Everyone who hoped to be chosen would stand behind a circle drawn by the Village Panchayat. The oracle would appear in the middle of the circle. But the hearts of the people living in Jinteroo village was filled with pride and greed, as their village was the only one with the entrance.

On the auspicious day, there was a human stampede on the outskirts of Jinteroo, fighting to get a spot to stand around the circle. There was no one alive who had experienced the Fountain's powers, and the ones who had, had departed to heaven, contented with their prosperity and happiness.

On the fifth day of the full moon, everyone stood in a queue and prepared to meet the oracle. As she was a goddess, the people had to prostrate before her and fold hands. Then the drums were heard and…

CRACCKKK!!!

The goddess appeared.

Everyone bowed. She walked near a boy, named Amit. Everyone thought, "He won't be selected. He is just a boy!"

The oracle sang her hymns and prayers, and tapped his head, TAP…!

The villagers thought, "That is only one tap. She will move on to someone else."

TAP…!

"No! It couldn't be!", the people's minds were racing!

TAP…!

The oracle showered the boy with flowers! And disappeared!

Everyone stared in amazement. His parents couldn't believe their luck! But they still cared for their little boy, and did not want him to get lost or get hurt in the deep, dark forest. "Amit is just eleven years old! He can't go alone!" said his father. "He will have to. It isss part of hisss karma" hissed a snake, and slithered away. Amit was a brave one. He beseeched his parents, "Mother and father, please let me go. I have been longing to go outside the village for many months. I might come back with lots of gifts." Saying thus, he hugged his parents.

Amit then swiftly ran home, and came back a few minutes later holding a knife, a woolen coat, some food and an egg. He pocketed the knife and the egg, wore the woolen coat, kept the food in a small bag and was ready to leave.

He bid his parents and fellow people goodbye and set out on his journey to the forest. He bravely entered the forest, and walked for a long time. Soon he reached the heart of the forest, and as his legs were tired, he sat down. He quickly ate the food and continued walking.

Soon he saw a light shining ahead. Thinking it must be the fountain, he ran towards it. Minutes later, he saw a strange creature. It was a monster! It had two wings, like a dragon, two long teeth like a Saber tooth tiger and, he realized the light was coming from a shiny red ruby on the head of the monster. Amit pulled the knife out of his pocket but didn't use it.

The monster roared, "I am the Dragontooth Monster. I shall eat you for I have been starving for eight years. I don't mind human flesh." Amit smiled, pocketed the knife, and gave the monster the rest of his food and his egg, and said, "Mr. Dragontooth, please eat this food. I am heading to the Fountain of Luck. If I get any food there, I shall share it with you."

The Monster was delighted. It had never been offered food before! It said, "Okay, you may go. I shall help you find your way there. Go straight till you find a cave. Don't go inside, but go around it so you will find a bush. Take a small peek above it, there you will see the Fountain of Peace."

And so, Amit thanked the Monster for the advice, bid farewell and went on his way. As the monster had told him to, Amit went straight ahead. There he found the cave, and went around it, and saw the bush. And then he saw—the Fountain!

The water pouring out of it was glistening, reflecting the beauty and splendor of the giant pearls, diamonds and rubies embedded on the rocks of the Fountain! Flowers, creepers and fruits encircled the Fountain as birds sang their calls, celebrating the wonder of the Fountain!

Amit was overwhelmed at the very sight of the Fountain. The birds encircled him, took his coat and started filling it with diamonds, sapphires and many gems. They filled his hands with yummy delicacies and soon, it was time to head back home. Amit had enough food and decided to leave.

On his way back, Amit remembered to visit the Dragontooth Monster, and gave it all the food it wanted, and skipped back home, feeling extremely happy and contented with life.

And so, my dear readers, let us all be like Amit—brave, confident, thoughtful and kind.

Even if there isn't a Fountain of Luck or a Dragontooth Monster to help us, our courage and smartness will take us to greater heights. Therefore, let's all aim for these qualities to achieve our goals.

And most importantly,

ALWAYS REMEMBER!!!—

When you embark on a journey, be sure to pack some extra food to carry along, because you never know when you will meet a hungry Dragontooth Monster.

Tanmayishri Sumanth

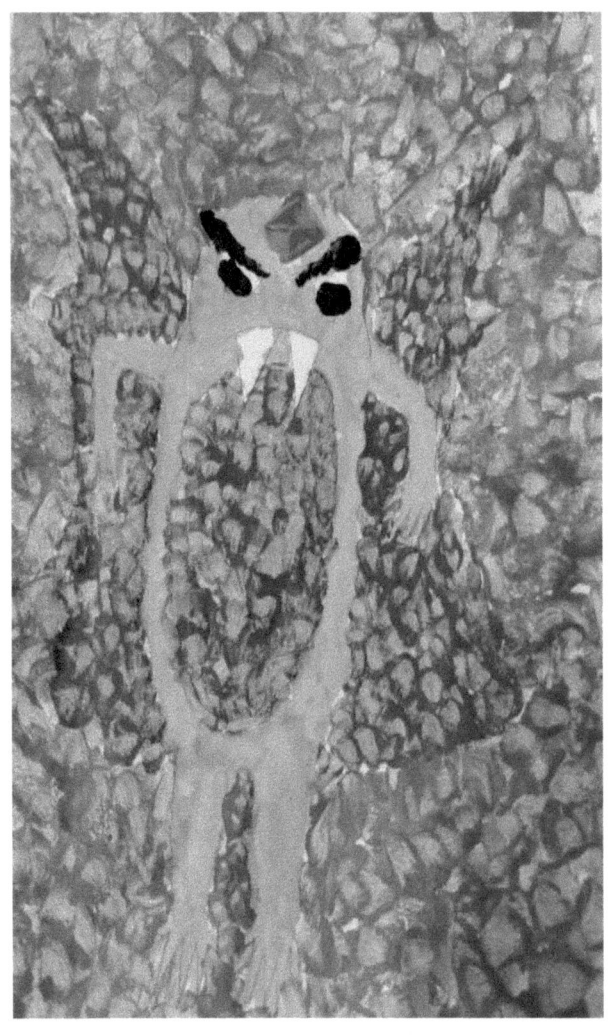

THE HUNGRY DRAGONTOOTH MONSTER

THE MAGIC CANYON

A long time ago, in a faraway land, there was a large, deep, deserted canyon. The canyon had many secrets and mysteries. People who went there were never to be seen again. They had completely vanished into thin air! Many archaeologists had entered and explored the canyon. And what became of them? No one knew! They never came back! The news spread around.

There was a valley a few miles away from the canyon. The people of the valley were suffering from a deadly disease. None of the doctors in the valley could cure it. There seemed to be no remedy!

Therefore, the villagers decided to try their luck. How? How does one find luck in such a dire situation? By being brave, of course! They planned to explore the canyon.

The idea was to send a few people and check if there were any useful medicinal herbs they could procure from the canyon. And so, they formed a group of the bravest and strongest men in the valley.

When they were about to depart, a boy named Arun stepped forward and said, "I could go with them, I want to explore the canyon." All the valley people, including his mother and father were worried, but they agreed that he was a brave and confident child. And thus, they let him go.

The troop departed, with bags full of food and water supplies. It was a very hot and sunny day. They walked for a long time, and soon, got to a huge tree. It was surrounded by pearls, diamonds and gems. All the men stared at the jewels in awe.

Did they dare touch it?

Not yet; they were hungry!

All of them sat and ate their snacks.

As they were about to leave, there heard a booming voice from above, "O people of the valley, I know why you have come. Look at all the gold around you. I advise you to grab all the gold you want, fill your bags and leave. Why walk all the way to the canyon?"

The people considered taking the advice, but Arun reminded them, "We have come here to find medicine for the disease. Do not get tempted by these attractive distractions. Let us focus on our aim and complete our duty first. We can always come back for the gold later, after we successfully complete our mission."

The men agreed, not because they weren't greedy, but because they were scared about the whole adventure in the first place! The troop continued on their journey.

A few minutes later, they found a table, laden with delicious food items. Pastries, cakes, ice creams, chocolate fountains, hot, roasted potatoes, Mexican noodles, tacos and a thousand other scrumptious varieties of delicacies! The mouths of the men began to water.

Arun again advised them to control their temptations and to keep walking. The people listened to him, because their stomachs were full.

Soon they reached the canyon. They couldn't see anything from outside. As they walked deeper into the canyon, LO AND BEHOLD! All the distracting objects they had seen were in front of their eyes! The diamonds and gold were lying in heaps! The food had doubled! And, much to their surprise and glee, the very particular medicine they needed was filled in seven large earthen pots.

Everyone enjoyed the food and took all the gold they could carry, and the precious medicine, too. Arun then understood that archeologists and other explorers who had come here before them, in the past, must have given in to their greed, and along the way they must have eaten all the food and took all the money. They must have been punished for their greed, which is why they never returned.

Stomachs full of food and arms loaded with the seven pots and lots of precious jewels, the troop returned to the valley. Everyone praised Arun for his advice that had led them to achieving their goals.

Suddenly, the voice, which the troop had heard earlier, said, "Arun, you have been wise. Hence, I crown you as 'Head of the Valley'. I bless you to be successful in life henceforth. Farewell."

Arun thanked the voice in his mind. And ever since, Arun has guided the people of the valley justly and wisely.

THE MAGIC CANYON

SHOES ON STRIKE!

We quit, humans!
You have treated us unfairly!
We shoes need to talk to you,
We should have mentioned it early!

We did, but you didn't listen,
To our tragic cries!
You walked on mud and dirt,
And who knows when it'll dry!

You wear us every day,
Whenever you go out,
Do you think we don't tell you?
Of course not; we scream and shout!

It wouldn't hurt, would it,
If you washed your pair of shoes,
Or be careful where you step on,
Because we have feelings too!

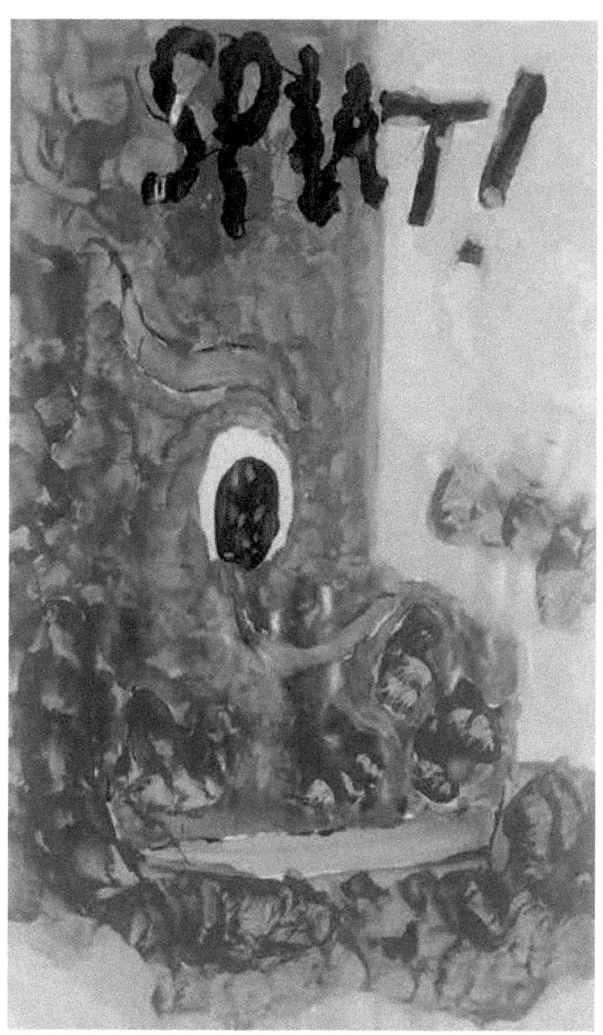

OOPS! YOU STEPPED ON DIRT...AGAIN!!!

THE CURSE OF A SAGE

Many years ago, in a dark forest, under a large banyan tree, on a flat stone, sat a sage, deep in meditation. For years and years, people had been coming to the forest, to pay their respects to the sage and give him some fruits and flowers. But the sage never opened his eyes to accept them.

One day, three men entered the forest looking for the sage. They intended to ask him for money. When they found the sage deep in meditation, they did not know what to do. One man was so restless that he kicked the sage.

The sage was startled, and angry too, but he hid it well, and pretended to be calm. He asked the men, "Why are you here, my dear men? I was only a BIT busy in meditation." The men were slightly confused with the sage's response, given the fact that one of them had actually kicked the sage. They told him that they have come to seek money from him. The sage replied, "I am only an ascetic. How can I give you money, when I myself starve without eating?"

The men retorted, "We know you are famous; and you have some kind of magic power. Give us a lot of gold." The sage said, "Alright. I will give you three wishes each. Use them carefully."

The men walked away eagerly, without thanking the sage. The first man told the other two, "I am going to find a restaurant and eat food for free, with my first wish. Will you come with me? The men agreed. And so, the three men enjoyed a hearty feast.

When it was time to pay, they said, "We wish to escape without paying for our meal." Nothing happened. What did happen was that they were forced to wash all the dishes and pay an expensive fine. They were thrown out of the restaurant. The first man scratched his head. How could the wish not work?

Anyway, the three tired men decided to book a taxi and go home. The first man used his second wish to ride the taxi for free and not pay the taxi driver. They took a taxi and had a quite relaxing ride. When it was time to pay the driver, the man said, "I wish not to pay the driver." The driver complained to the police that the men did not pay the money after the ride, and so, again, the poor men were forced to pay a fine with whip lashes.

The first man was so frustrated, he said, "I wish the other two men's wishes would atleast work!" And so, the first man's third wish got used up too. The next day, it was the second man's turn to make a wish.

The men decided to rent a mansion for themselves. The went to the renting shop and the second man made a wish that they wouldn't have to pay money for it. They took the key and turned around. As they were about to leave— "OY! Where are you going? Pay the money!" The men ran away, but eventually, they were caught. They were given ten lashes each and were sent home.

The second man wished that the pain, the scars on his body caused, would go. But, it didn't. The man used his third wish to make three water bottles appear on the desk, one for each of them. But that didn't happen.

The first and second man had wasted their three wishes, but the third man was adamant not to. The next day, they all went to the village festival. The third man wished first that they wouldn't have to pay money, and took a lot of food from the stalls without paying money. When the shopkeepers asked for the money, he used his second wish and wished they would escape from the police. But just as he said it out loud, the police heard him, and pursued them.

The three men were put in jail, for they had committed too many crimes. The third man used his third and final wish and wished they would be set free, but that only made the guard even more alert!

And, guess what? The sage had actually NOT GRANTED them any wishes! As one of the men had kicked him, and the greedy men demanded money and gold...the sage had only mentioned empty wishes to teach them a lesson!

And so, we learn from this story that we will be treated in the same manner as to how we treat others!

THE MEDITATING SAGE

THE PRINCE AND THE CAVE

A long time ago, far away, in a misty land, there was a cave. It was an old cave, made of thick boulders. No one ever dared to enter the cave, because the people who did venture near the cave were never to be seen again.

People believed that a monster lived inside the mysterious cave, and it had killed and eaten the people, which is why they never returned. But the monster never stepped out of the cave, and no one knew why.

A few miles away from the cave, there was a kingdom. It was ruled by a just king named Dharmasena, his wife Lilavati, and his heir, a young prince named Sriniketh.

Sriniketh was the crown prince of the kingdom, and was brave, strong and adventurous. The whole kingdom knew about the cave and the monster, and so did Sriniketh.

Prince Sriniketh wanted to get rid of the monster, but his parents were afraid for him, as the cave was a dangerous place. However, after the recent news of the death of three men who ventured into the cave, king Dharmasena reluctantly agreed for the prince to go.

As soon as they gave him permission to go and fight the monster, the prince ran to his chamber and pulled out an old chest from his almirah. The chest contained his late grandfather's armour, including a pair of magic boots. Queen Lilavati had told him that a long ago, an angel had appeared and given his grandfather the boots, and that they would give the owner or the wearer lots of courage.

The king and queen prayed for his safe return, and the prince left in his chariot. Soon they reached the entrance of the cave. The heroic prince got off, and the charioteer rode back to the kingdom.

"Krrrrr...Shhh...Krrrrr... Shhh..."

The prince became curious as he heard weird sounds coming from inside the cave! Determined to find the source of the sound, he went inside and saw, much to his shock, skeletons and blood of many animals and humans!

And there, sleeping and snoring loudly was a humungous, golden tiger, with wings like that of a dragon! And smoke was coming out of its' nostrils!

The prince had neither seen nor heard of anything like this before! He valiantly walked near it and raised his sword. "SHRINNN!", came the noise as the prince slashed the sword. He cut off the tiger's head!

"I killed the monster. That was so easy!" He thought.

Just then, CLICK!

The tiger's head had attached itself to the body! The Tiger-headed Dragon-winged Monster roared loudly and half-pounced and half-flew towards the prince.

The prince dodged its powerful claws and hit the monster hard with his sword. The cave echoed with a sharp cry, and then, there was utter silence. Finally, the monster fell back, dead.

Just then, the prince heard a serene voice, "Dear prince, I am the king of the heavens! I appreciate your valour. The monster had a boon that nothing could kill it in their first attack! As a reward for your bravery, please, accept this gold as a reward." Thus spoke the angel his mother had told him about!

"Oh, angel, that would be unfair. It is because of the courage my boots gave me that I could slay that monster," said the prince. The angel replied," Your grandfather's boots are not magical."

"Whaaat! So did my mother lie to me about you?" Sriniketh interrupted, shocked.

The angel felt insulted, and retorted, "Boy! I'm not a lie! I'm talking to you! Look at your feet! Those boots don't even fit you!"

(Dear readers, if you don't believe that the boots don't fit the prince, check the illustration for this story.)

The angel continued, "It is YOUR courage that helped you kill the monster. Not those lumpy old boots! Now, just accept those precious things". Sacks of pearls, diamonds and gold appeared near him.

Prince Sriniketh took the gifts and returned to the kingdom, and narrated to his mother and father all that had occurred. The king and queen were proud of their son's victorious return, and Dharmasena made him the king. Sriniketh ruled wisely for many, many years to come.

A Treasure Trove of Tales

PRINCE SRINIKETH IN HIS LUMPY BOOTS

THE DIVINE POWER

Long back, many thousand centuries ago, Lord Brahma was creating the Earth. It was very important work. As he wanted to make human beings, later to be known as his best creation, he worked very hard at it and also decided to gift humans with powers.

But there was a small problem. The powers were kept in a large, decorated box. They zoomed around inside the box, trying to get out of the box and into one of Lord Brahma's creations. Brahma was worried one of the powers might escape. If they did, the first living thing they touched would get the power!

So, he carefully took the box, created man and gave them the powers to speak, move, see, hear and touch. He then created woman and gave them similar powers. As he was creating a girl, he FORGOT to close the box, and— ZOOP!

A tiny power zoomed out and entered the girl's eyes. Lord Brahma spied it, but he could not do anything about it. He sent the girl to her mother's womb, and wondered what the power could do. Yes, even he did not know what magic would happen!

By the way, the girl was named Anu and her mother was a lady named Lila. Anu grew up to be a graceful and kind person. But when she turned eight years, she was having problems at school with a bully named Vindi.

As Anu boarded the school bus, Vindi quietly opened her school bag's zip and took out Anu's lunch box. Anu started running after him and snatched it from his hands. Anu was so angry, she wished she could hit him!

She suddenly heard someone whisper, "May the power be with you." And the next moment she was filled with confidence. Now, she could stand up to Vindi!

She looked back and saw something she had never seen before. Right before her, there were many little fairies. *'Or were they?'* and they were wearing tiaras and shawls.

Anu was thunderstruck! The angels, [that's who they were] were alarmed. They all realized Anu could see them and started flying away even as Anu called back. But a little angel stopped. She waved her wand and spoke, 'You mustn't be able to see us. How can you?'

Anu was shocked. 'Oh, other children can't see you? Then she noticed that Vindi was still there. He teased Anu, 'Who are you talking to? An invisible force?' The other fairies waved their wands and Vindi suddenly fell back as though somebody kicked him.

Anu giggled, as Vindy ran as fast as he could the opposite way. The angels smiled and said softly,' That's what we're supposed to do, teach lessons to people like him!'

Anu said 'Thanks! Oh, and I must be off, everyone's left!' And so, Anu bustled of into the crowd, excited to tell her mother Lila all that had happened. As she rang the doorbell, her mother soon appeared, wearing a gown and a frown.

'You're late!' she snapped. 'What took you so long? The food is cold. Come and eat!'

Anu said, 'Mummy, you will not believe what I just saw!' Anu narrated everything in detail and answered every question Lila asked.

Then Lila's mind began to work fast. She said, 'This little power of yours could get us a lot of fame! I hope you aren't fibbing to get my attention!'

Anu said, 'But Mummy, instead of telling everyone about my powers, won't it be better to keep it a secret, so no one feels jealous? I mean'—

But Lila wasn't listening. She was busy calling her friends to tell them about Anu's powers. Soon, days flew past.

Everyone was tired of Lila's continuous chatter. Soon, her friends began to stop speaking with her. Anu was unhappy her mother did not listen to her in the first place.

She told Lila, 'Mummy, you can try saying sorry to everyone that you bragged to, but first I will try to remove the power. I so wish to be normal, like everyone else.'

Just then a voice said, 'O little girl, you have been unselfish. You expressed the desire to get rid of the power. I will remove the power. I thus also grant you a wish.' It was Lord Brahma speaking.

Anu said, 'My Lord, I only wish that my mother is forgiven for her bragging. Thank you for your kindness, Lord Brahma.'

Anu decided to write a story about her adventures and pastimes. And that is what you have been reading now!

A Treasure Trove of Tales

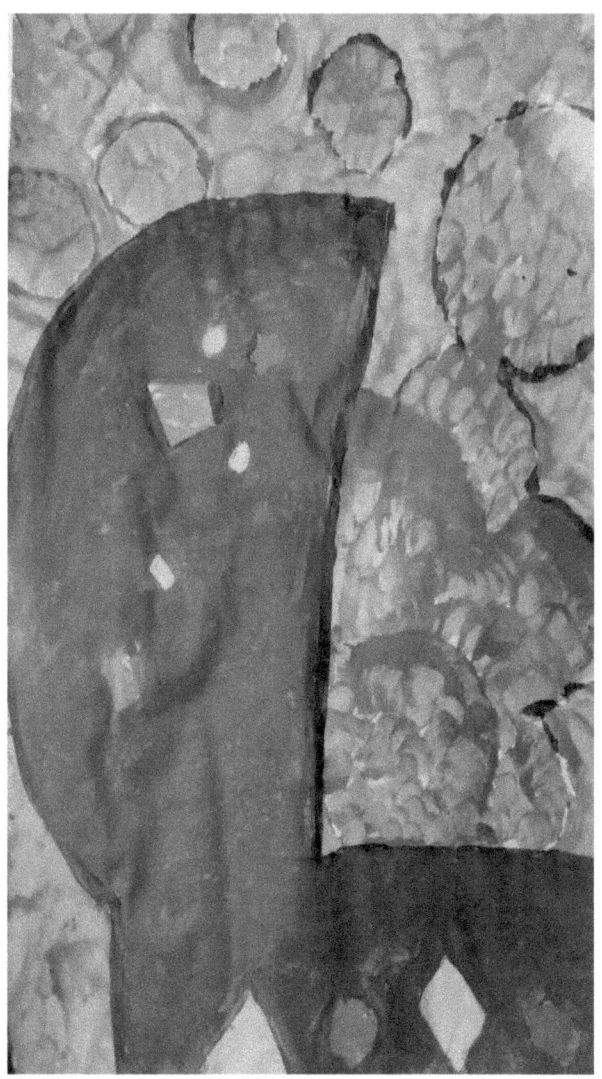

THE BOX OF POWERS

THE ISHAVRIKSHA TRIBE

I DEDICATE THIS STORY TO MY DAD
(I'll let you know why at the end)

In a small village in a faraway country, there was a friendly native tribe named Ishavriksha. People liked to settle in the village because the tribe had planted many trees that provided juicy fruits.

One day, when the tribe had gone to the forest on a hunt, a terrible incident occurred. A giant horrible monster came across the group of men as they were walking; he picked them up like tiny ants and threw them all into a large bag, tied the knot with ropes, carried them along and went his way. The tribe didn't return to the village.

The news soon reached the villagers. All of them liked the good, hardworking tribe. Also, all of them were scared that they would be eaten by the monster someday. The head of the village organized a meeting with all the villagers, so they could save the tribe. Despite being strong and brave, none of the men had the courage to go to rescue the tribe.

As they were about to give up, someone said, "O people of the village, I would be glad to help the tribe. I will return safely". It was the voice of a brave, kind little girl, named Anita. The people were worried, for she was only a child, but when they looked at her bright, confident little face, they agreed for her to go.

Anita ran to her house, and brought a bag full of food, water, and a knife, which she put in her pocket. She started walking towards the West, which was the way the tribe went earlier. After a few minutes, she reached a shrine of Lord Buddha. She prostrated before the idol and prayed, "O Lord, please bless me to return safely with the tribe. I believe your

Divine Grace will surely help me in the journey. Thank you."

Saying thus she continued on her way. Alas! What was in front of her! There was a bed of hard, sharp-edged rocks! Then a voice came, "Anita, feel in your pockets. There is a paper plane. Jump on it, and it will take you to the place of the monster." Anita felt her pocket. There was the knife she had kept earlier, and— SURPRISE!

A paper plane!   POOF!

The plane flew out and expanded in size. Anita sat on it and it soared out into the sky! After an hour, the plane landed softly on the ground, and vanished.

Anita walked for some time and then found a prison. Inside it, there were twenty cells. Anita noticed that the cells had no guards. Locked inside each cell was a tribal person. She tried opening the locks, slashing them with her knife.

One of the tribe's men said, "It is of no use, dear girl. The bars are made of iron, they cannot be cut easily. You need the key. It is guarded by the monster, which is sleeping now. Go around my cell, and you will find the monster."

Anita thanked the tribal man and did as he said. Sure enough, she found the monster, snoring loudly. She tiptoed past the monster, and found a chest. Inside it, there was the key. She took it and went back to the cells, freed all the tribal men. And, hoping that the monster would never disturb the tribe or anyone else ever again, she slit the throat of the monster, when—

LO AND BEHOLD!

The monster disappeared, and in its place stood a—

Wait!!!

Dear readers, what do you think stood in place of the monster?

Maybe a beautiful princess or a handsome knight?

We all have monsters in us, right?

It could be envy, jealousy, hatred or anger— Anything!

When we face it with bravery, it disappears— POOF!

And in our story, Anitha and the tribal men saw that in place of the monster, now stood a delicious, creamy, chocolate cake!

The cake said joyfully, "I was once a regular cake, but an evil witch tried to eat me. When I hopped away from her plate, she got angry. I said that I only enter the mouths of good people, and called her a bad nut. She cursed me to become a monster. I begged and begged her to take the curse off, but she wouldn't budge. I hopped over to a good fairy's cottage. The kind lady said she couldn't remove the entire curse, as her powers were limited. But she said I would be a cake again after someone, brave and unselfish, slit my throat. And now I am relived from that hideous form! Please devour my luscious creams, dear girl! And you too, noble sirs!", the cake addressed the tribal men.

They devoured the cake graciously. Anita, the Ishavriksha tribe and bits of the cake in their tummies returned to the village cheerily. All the villagers praised Anita for her courage and bravery, and therefore knighted her, Anita the Brave.

By the way, I dedicate this story to my dad, not because he is brave, or that he is a tribal man. It is because—

HE LOVES CHOCOLATE CAKE!

IT WAS ALL THANKS TO BUDDHA THAT THE TRIBE RETURNED SAFELY!

THE BRAVE KING

Once upon a time, in a large palace, there lived a king. His palace's architecture was exquisitely beautiful and the structure was immensely accurate. The king lived a contented and prosperous life. The gold, jewels, diamonds and pearls in his treasury were unlimited! He was brave, courageous and straightforward. All his people were inspired by him and wanted to be like him.

Nevertheless, there was one thing everyone was afraid of. It was a monster, which came twice in a year, on a full moon day. It would come to the palace and eat a quarter of the kingdom's population.

The king was worried that one day, his whole kingdom would be eaten. So, he decided that he would fight the monster and protect his kingdom.

On the day before the full moon, he set out in search of the monster, taking his shield, sword, and a map of the outskirts, his armour clanking loudly as he walked. He bid goodbye to his subjects and galloped away on his horse. He looked at his map. He'd have to cross the forest, and pass a large tree, to reach the den of the monster.

He steered the horse forward, and reached the middle of the forest after a few hours. It was getting dark. Dusk was falling. So, he decided to sleep under a tree, for the night. But just as he got off his horse, it started raining! He took his sword, cut a large hole on the tree trunk, and climbed inside it. Minutes later, he was sound asleep.

In the morning, when he woke up, he was surprised to find himself and his horse in the outskirts of the kingdom!

He wondered, "Did anyone bring me here?" Then, he heard a voice. "I am the king of the angels. The forest, is a deep, dark and dangerous place. The monster disturbs the angels too. We all want your victory in killing the monster. Hence, we helped you cross the forest."

The king thanked the king of angels, and climbed on his horse once again. After an hour, he reached a cave.

As soon as he entered the cave, GRRROWL! He then saw the scariest creature ever! It had five heads, three eyes and four hands! Also, it had dragon wings and, to the king's shock, was breathing fire!

"I am the Bloodsucker, the most vicious of my kind! I feel like I have been starving for centuries despite raiding kingdoms on the night of full moon. And now, it is not I, who have found my dessert, but my dessert has come to me!" The monster roared gleefully, and lashed its fangs at the king.

Before the king could pull out his sword from the sheath, the Bloodsucker lunged forward at him, and moments later, killed him.

Wait a minute, the hero can't die!

Hmmm…

The story isn't over yet!

Just then, many tiny little angels and their very majestic angel king appeared and pierced the beast all over his body with their little swords. The angel king revived the other king with a life-saving potion.

With one move of his sword, the revived king chopped off the head of the great brute. Finally, with a scream of agony, the great brute was finished.

All of them returned to their homes, without a single worry in their mind.

A Treasure Trove of Tales

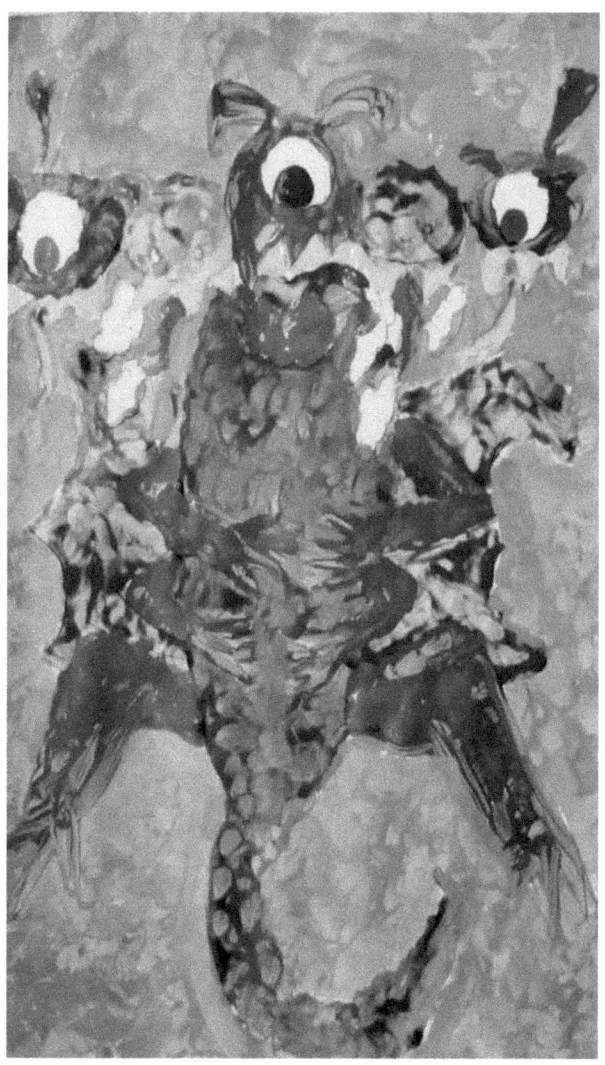

THE BLOODTHIRSTY BLOODSUCKER

DEEP IN THE JUNGLE

Deep in the jungle,
As dark as dark can be,
Lie wild animals,
Hidden amongst leaves

Deep in the jungle,
In a lion's den,
Are the lion and lioness,
Snacking on dead men.

Deep in the jungle,
Is a parakeet,
Sitting on the branch,
Of an enormous tree.

Deep in the jungle,
Aiming at a stag,
Are three hunters, behind a bush,
They've got this one in the bag!

Deep in the jungle,
Swinging from tree to tree,
Making loud noises,
Are four monkeys.

Deep in the jungle,
Sitting on a log,
Are two fat toads,
And a slimy frog.

Going on a pilgrimage,
Are two travellers,
Perched on a tree, chatting
Are two blue birds.

One bird says, sadly,
"Those men are in for a shock."
The other one asks, "Why?
They are just heading for the dock."

The first bird replied, "Yonder is a tiger,
If they proceed, they will not survive."
And sure enough, there was one,
The poor travellers wouldn't be alive!

The jungle is a dangerous place,
Full of horrible things,
Even if you have soldiers to protect you,
Even if you are a king!

A Treasure Trove of Tales

THE TWO BLUE BIRDS

THE WATERMELON TREE

[DEDICATED TO ALL THE SCIENCE TEACHERS IN THE WORLD]

Do watermelons grow on trees?

No, they are creepers.

They don't talk, either.

But who's complaining?

It's just a story! So, let's enjoy it!

In a garden, there was a large, big tree. It had many leaves and branches. It had a large, big Watermelon hanging from a large, big branch. But Watermelon was very scared, for he was afraid of heights. He shuddered to think what would happen if he fell down!

All of Watermelon's friends (the other fruits) were eager for Watermelon to come down, as they wanted to play with him.

Every day, they came to his garden and said,

>"Friend Watermelon,
>
>Please come down.
>
>Come happily without a frown,
>
>Let's play kings and queens wearing a gown,
>
>And march all around the town!"

Watermelon always refused, but one day he replied—

>"Then please, come, my friends,
>
>With a ladder!
>
>I then shall enjoy,
>
>Without becoming sadder!"

Cherry cried, "Oh, yes, we shall!"

And, all the fruits together brought a ladder from their garage, and called —

"My dear friend Watermelon,
We are back!
Come down!
Let's play with a railway track!"

Watermelon looked down, and screamed,
"Oh, look, I am so high!
I realize I'm almost touching the sky!
I am sorry to trouble you on and on,
Please do bring a bed for me to land on!"

Pineapple ran to his house, and came back, pulling along a big bed and a toy car. He called out,
"Look at this, Watermelon dear,
There is no need to fear!
Come down fast, and let's enjoy!
Let's play with my new toy!"

Watermelon looked down again, and said, "But what if I fall down?"

Pineapple reassured, "No, you won't! I positioned this bed exactly right. You will only fall in the middle."

But at that moment, Watermelon thought, Apple has a fire truck! Why don't I ask him to bring it?

And so, Watermelon said,

"Apple, Apple, your fire truck,

Bring it, let's try our luck!"

Apple said, "I am too tired to drive, Watermelon. Please come down."

Then, Banana remembered that Watermelon's greatest fear was of cats.

And, very cleverly, Banana yelled— "Look, guys! There is a CAT!"

The moment Watermelon heard the word "Cat", he hopped right out of his branch, right onto the soft bed!

For a moment, everyone was silent.

When Mango yelled, "Excellent, Watermelon! You've come out of your tree!", everyone realized that watermelon had indeed come down from the tree top.

And everyone clapped for Watermelon, for he had overcome his fear! And all of them enjoyed the company of Watermelon heartily, and Watermelon enjoyed theirs too!

THE WATERMELON SITTING ON HIS TREE

THE ANIMALS AND THE MONSTER

On the foot of a large mountain, was a forest. The forest was full of trees, for the arboreal animals like monkeys and squirrels, surrounded by greenery. There were many fresh water sources for the fishes and water dwellers, and very fertile soil, for the animals that lived underground. All of the animals lived cozily in their comfortable homes within the vast forest.

Unfortunately, a few miles away from the forest, lived a menacing monster. The monster grabbed many animals from the forest, and put them in cages.

After it had collected many animals, it would take them out and boil them in water. Then the vile menace would eat the poor animals!

All the animals locked up were trying to come up with a way of escaping their gruesome death. They got tensed whenever the monster shouted at his poor servant, like this—

"Hey, Ho!

Run and go,

Fetch me a cup of water!

Boil it to make it hotter!

So, heat it, quick!

Or your bones I shall lick!"

One day, the Owl said, "Bear, you are very strong. Why don't you break open your cage, and keep those bottles of wine near the monster on the ground? He will be tempted and will drink them all in one go. Then, Hare could go and ask him to free us from these cages. Absent mindedly, he will unlock the cages and we will run back home."

Bear and Hare agreed. Everyone praised Owl's clever plan, and encouraged Hare and Bear to do as Owl asked.

And everything worked out, just as planned! The monster freed everyone, and as they ran home—

"ROAAARRRRR!"

The monster realized what it had done, and it sure wasn't happy about it! The monster's every step shook the ground and made trees fall! All the animals ran for their lives. But Owl's plan never went wrong! Ha!

The wine was actually poisoned, and so—

CCCRRAAAASHH!

The monster fell down, dead.

Everyone was quiet.

Suddenly—YIPPEEEE!!!!
Everyone rejoiced.

All the animals celebrated the death of their great enemy, and they crowned Owl the king! And, from that day, the animals lived peacefully, without a worry in the world!

THE WISE OWL IN THE CAGE

AHA, OHO AND HEHE

There were once three tricksters named Aha, Oho and Hehe. Together they would travel to many villages and kingdoms to rob people and cheat them.

One day they arrived at the kingdom of a wise and great emperor named Anantasena.

Aha suggested, "Aha! There is a rich king by the name Anantasena. We can pretend to be his minister and fool him. Then, we can rob him!"

Oho exclaimed, "Oho! We can get the whole treasury! I agree!"

Hehe laughed, "Hehe! You both are being foolish; we cannot rob the treasury that easily!

We need to be careful. The treasury is guarded by soldiers. So, stop dreaming and let's get to work!"

The trio walked past the gates of the empire and soon reached the gates of the palace. They were blocked by two guards. A guard looked at them suspiciously. The other guard asked, "Who are you, and for what purpose have you come to this empire?"

Oho thought, "Let me give some good remarks about their emperor. The guards will be flattered and will allow us to enter." Thinking thus, Oho answered, "Oho! We have come because we want to serve the great, majestic emperor."

Aha thought, "We will have to gain some time to get our hands in the treasury, so I will tell them we are gifted men." Thus, Aha said, "Aha! And we want the pleasure of entertaining the emperor. We are very talented men. Give us an opportunity to show our great talents to the emperor!" Hehe chuckled quietly.

The guards let them pass, and escorted them to the court, where the mighty emperor Anantasena sat, on his majestic golden throne, with silver lions on each side of it.

The emperor asked, "Hello, my dear men! Please tell me why you have come to me."

Aha said, "Aha! Your majesty, we have come to serve you. We are extremely talented. I, Aha, can… ummm… erm…find things that are lost. I can find many objects that people lost in about five minutes!"

Oho cried, "Oho! I can do even better! I…errr… am a very watchful, alert and observant person! I am good at guarding precious things, like gold! Not a single insect or person, neither an ant nor an elephant can escape my attentive eye!"

Hehe remarked, "Aha and Oho have useful talents, but I am… excellent at entertaining! I can crack a limitless number of jokes and puns! I am extremely hilarious and fun to be with!"

Hehe's claims picked Anantasena' s interest and the king said, "You can tell jokes. Can you? Now, tell me a joke about food and time!" Hehe scratched his head. "I… Errr… Ok. Here's one. Seven days without food makes one 'weak'. The emperor angrily said, "That was really bad! It wasn't funny!"

Hehe replied, "Er... You see, your majesty, a week without food DOES make a person weak... Me and my friends haven't eaten in days! We are tired. I cannot make good jokes unless I am fed well. You might become fed up of my jokes, if I'm not fed!"

The emperor chuckled. He told them, "You may take rest for a few hours here. I will ensure you get a chamber (which were rooms, in the olden days) filled with necessities like food and clothes."

Aha, Oho and Hehe asked the emperor for a job in the palace so they may stay permanently. Anantasena agreed, and gave each of them a job.

Aha was given the job of finding lost property of the citizens ("Aha!"). Oho (much to his delight) was made the treasurer, ("Oho..."), and Hehe was the court jester ("Hehe!"). Anantasena told them they would be given three gold coins each, for a month's work, if they did their job properly.

After the trio were given a place to stay, Oho rejoiced at his luck of being the treasurer, for now it was the easiest job to steal the gold! The next day, they all went to their respective places at the court. Oho went to the treasury, and, as soon as he was out of sight, began shovelling the gold in to his pockets greedily. After his pockets were full of gold, he decided it was enough for the day.

As soon as he walked out, a courtier saw his pockets bulging with gold, and, just as a coin dropped out of it, the courtier grabbed him by the hand and dragged Oho to the emperor, telling him how Oho had emerged out of the treasury with stolen gold.

The angry emperor Anantasena threw Oho out of the empire and made another honest man his treasurer. An injured, grumbling Oho made his way to a faraway place. Eventually, Aha and Hehe learned what happened to Oho, and ran away from the empire. They sure learnt a lesson from this experience!

Praise and comforts come from real talent, and hard work!

One cannot fake his true identity forever, because one's true intentions are bound to come out in one's actions!

AHA OHO AND HEHE—THE TRICKSTERS

THE CLEVER MINISTER

Many years ago, in a faraway land, there was once a loyal chief minister named Suryadev. He served a brave, kind and humble king named Chandrasena. Suryadev was very witty and clever, and could see the good in everyone.

Chandrasena was grateful and pleased to have such a wise man for his minister, and would treat him as an equal, spending his leisure time with Suryadev. At times, when they took a stroll in the royal garden, they would have deep conversations about life.

One day, Chandrasena received a message from the neighbouring king, proposing his daughter's hand in marriage to a man who performs three tasks given by the queen. The princess was an exquisitely beautiful maiden, with soft hands and a lovely voice. She was worth a thousand tasks! But the three given tasks were rather strange!

King Chandrasena showed the message to Suryadev, and said, "The first task is a jumping competition. Among all suitors, the man who jumps the highest is qualified to attempt the next task. Then, the queen will present a sack of grains and will scatter them all over the floor. The suitor who picks up all the grains and puts them in the bag within an hour wins this round! The third and final task is a yelling competition! The man who shouts the loudest wins the princess's hand!"

Chandrasena said, "I have a queen, but you might be able to accomplish the tasks and marry the princess, with your clever skills!"

Suryadev agreed to go to the neighbouring kingdom to try his luck. Therefore, the very next day he set out on his beautiful white horse and galloped away!

On his way, Suryadev met a man who was tying heavy boulders and rocks on his foot. Suryadev stopped to ask, "Doesn't your feet hurt, my dear man, with such heavy stones on them?"

The man sadly replied, "I am Hopfoot. I am bound to tie these seemingly heavy objects to my feet, else I will fly away! I am more than outstanding at jumping! Even if I just raise my feet a bit, I can reach the sky! I am gripping the hard ground with my toes! I am so light that I can reach the stars without a rocket! Look, these ropes are tightening, my legs are pulling to untie themselves!" And he was right! He seemed very disturbed when the ropes tightened.

Suryadev thought, "The jumping competition! He seems outstanding at it! If I manage to befriend Hopfoot, I could win the competition!"

Suryadev helped Hopfoot stand up, and assured him, "My friend, I will help you if you come with me, and help me in a competition, I can buy you large suction boots that pull you to the ground!"

Hopfoot gladly agreed. Soon the duo reached a river. There was a man holding a glass box full of tiny little ants, and he was talking to them! Suryadev was about to walk further, but suddenly, he thought, "Wait! There was a grain picking competition! The ants have small hands and are an expert at it! The man could ask them to help me!"

He asked, "My friend, I see you have a talent, talking to ants! Could you do me a favour by coming with me, and help me finish a task? I shall give you seven gold *mohurs*!" The man gladly agreed, and introduced himself as Antmouth. As Suryadev was very tired, they all sat under a tree to rest.

Suddenly—

AAAAAAAAAAARRRRRRGGGH!!!

Someone was screaming like a dying duck! Suryadev ran to the place where the voice came from. A man was sitting on a bench, massaging his throat. Suryadev was about to shout at the man, for yelling like that, but then he remembered, "The yelling competition! This man is perfect!"

Suryadev realized the competition would start in ten minutes, so he quickly requested the man (who was called Highthroat) to come along with him. He promised to pay the man ten golden bars. Highthroat considered the request, and finally agreed.

The four men (Suryadev, Hopfoot, Antmouth and Highthroat) quickly headed to the neighbouring king's palace. They were just in time for the competition! The king announced, "Let the jumping competition begin!"

All the suitors could stay in the air only for two seconds. After a few minutes, it was Suryadev's turn. He asked Hopfoot to do the needful. Hopfoot stretched his legs and—

SPROING!

He had disappeared into the clouds! After three hours, Hopfoot landed on the palace ground! Everyone was astounded. Hopfoot won!

The king then announced, "Next up is the grain picking competition." Suryadev instructed Antmouth about the rules of the task. Antmouth opened his glass box open and whispered in the ant language—

Sss... Shhh... Sss...

If you don't know ant language, here is the translation— "Pick the grains and put them in that sack". In no more than twenty seconds, not one grain was left on the ground!

The astonished king said, "Let's begin the yelling competition." Everyone put on their earmuffs. It was going to be loud! Highthroat was first in line.

One... Two... Three...

AAAAARRRRRGGGGHHHHHHH!!!!

The king and queen winced. Highthroat was the winner! And that's how Suryadev married the princess.

All of the three helpers returned with Suryadev to Chandrasena's palace with their gifts—Hopfoot with his suction boots, Antmouth with his gold *mohurs*, Highthroat with the golden bars, and Suryadev with his new wife!

YOU'D BETTER WEAR YOUR EARMUFFS...

HIGHTHROAT IS YELLING!

THE FLYING VEENA

Dedicated to all the Music teachers in the world!

Far away, in a misty valley, sat a swami. He had been immersed in meditation for many months. There was a village near the place where the swami sat. People would come from the village to where the swami sat and would give him lots of food.

One day, after the swami completed his meditation, he opened his eyes and saw the people. The people said, "O divine swami, please bless us with musical talent. Our village is a barren place without it. Could you please gift us with a good voice?"

The swami would never say a no to people who were sincerely devoted to him. So, the swami raised his hands, and—

FLASH!!!

— a blinding light flashed upon where the swami sat.

POOF!

The swami disappeared. In the place where he sat lay a veena, shining in the rays of the sun.

The people were confused. They tried singing. Their voice hadn't changed a bit.

Suddenly, CRASH!

Everyone was shocked!

The veena had shot up like a firebolt and broke a branch of the tree above!

It was flying!

There it was, hovering above their heads, like a helicopter!

After few moments, it flew away! The people ran after it. They ran to the neighbouring village, right into a backyard of a man and found him playing it.

(In case you are wondering what happened, the veena flew into the man's backyard and he had exclaimed, "Wow! Such a beautiful instrument!", and had started playing it.)

They tried to take it from him. The man hesitated, but the veena shook itself out of the man's hands, shot up again and started diving towards the ground.

Oh no! The villagers screamed, "Somebody CATCH IT! It'll break!"

Oh no! It was too late!

The veena bashed itself to pieces. The people felt terrible. Suddenly, they heard a loud, yet calm voice. Where did it come from? No one knew! It seemed to come from everywhere.

The ground as well as the people's hearts vibrated as it spoke, "Dear people of this village, I am indeed sorry you lost your veena. Musical talent cannot be created by magic, it comes with practice. The flying veena was my creation. The swami was an illusion. I had to teach you that if you practice a lot, you will learn to sing. Practice makes a person perfect, and hard work leads to success."

The people understood their mistake. They burnt the broken veena, and divided the holy ash among themselves. The essence of the ash increased their confidence!

All of them practiced for many months, and after a year, they all became great singers.

Tanmayishri Sumanth

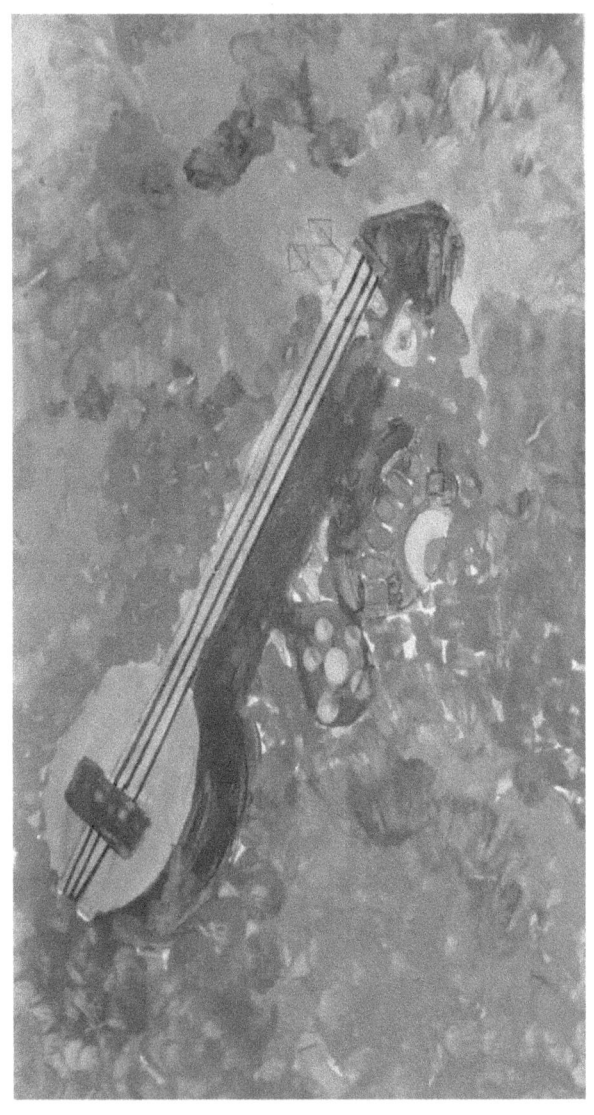

THE FLYING VEENA

ON THE NIGHT OF HALLOWEEN

On a very dark night,
Rather misty too,
There comes many a bright light,
From windows of houses, few.

As a boy sniffs in the air,
He exclaims, rubbing his belly,
"Chocolate eclairs, Gummy bears!
And lots of strawberry jelly!"

All the children come,
To many, many gates,
Of many, many houses,
With their classmates.

It's the trick- or- treating hour!
Ding- Dong! Rings the bell,
"Hello!" Answers a kind voice,
"Aren't you dressed well?"

She offered the kids some toast,
And asked them to sit down,
"Thanks a lot!" says the ghost,
Wearing a fake frown!

With pumpkin lanterns,
Lighting up the streets,
The happy children go back home,
With boxes full of treats!

A Treasure Trove of Tales

TRICK OR TREAT?

THE PUMPKIN JUICE MYSTERY

Dedicated to all the English, Hindi & Math teachers in the world!

There was peace and quiet in Number Village. Everybody was doing their own business, and no one ever needed help.

Hundred, the mayor, was going to the next village, Alpha Village, to meet their mayor, Z. They both shook hands. Then they sat down to talk.

Hundred was confused. Z had called him urgently to the village. Everything seemed ok! What was the problem?

Z looked very worried. He sadly said, "We have a problem in our village, Hundred. Everybody is falling asleep."

Hundred said, "But that is usual! Everybody needs to sleep!"

Z said, "No, no, you have misunderstood. They are all falling asleep in the daytime, too. Every time they drink pumpkin juice, I noticed."

Did you know, pumpkin juice is actually energizing?

Yes!

But how could the pumpkin juice in this story make everyone fall asleep?

Read on and find out!

Hundred said, "Aha! Maybe there is a pumpkin juice swapper! He takes everybody's glasses of juice, when they aren't looking. He grabs a bottle of sleeping potion, and mixes it in the pumpkin juice. The person, unaware of what is in his hand, drinks the mixture, and falls asleep!"

Z exclaimed, "Oh, Hundred, it is amazing, the way you found this out! But how do we find the mischief maker?"

Hundred thought for a moment, and then said, "We can give everyone a glass of pumpkin juice, and see who refuses it. The one who put the sleeping potion into the pumpkin juice would be very cautious not to drink it, and so we would find our culprit!

Make sure you give the juice to everyone, even in other places like Multiplication City, Division Town, Word Mountain, Sentence Valley etc. The thief could be hiding anywhere!"

Z clapped his hands in excitement, and agreed. By the next day, 10,000,000 glasses of juice were ready. Mayor Z's servants were busy, distributing them. After four and a half hours, everyone had a glass of juice in hand.

After another hour, thirty tired servants came, dragging along with them all the Hindi letters from their village. All of them were sweating, kicking and pummeling the servants to let them go.

"So here are our culprits!", exclaimed Z, cheerfully!

The Hindi letters were sorry they had done this. They said, "We did this because none of the students think this subject is important. Even if it isn't their mother tongue, we are still important.

For example, if you want to eat a chaat item in Delhi, you will need to know Hindi to converse with the shopkeeper, or the chaat might become too spicy or too sweet!

We are really important! To solve this problem, we planned to make you sleepy so the students would be bored studying you, and would give more importance to Hindi. We are extremely sorry."

Hundred told Z, "Well, I think they really repent for their actions. Will you let them go?" Z nodded.

The Hindi letters went back to Hindi Village, and Hundred was happy the problem was solved once and for all. All was well in the Alpha Village once again.

So, you can go drink your pumpkin juice without any fear!

A GLASS OF PUMPKIN JUICE

THE APPLIANCE STORE ADVENTURE

Dedicated To All the Computer Science Teachers in The World!!!

It was quite a boring day at the appliance store. It might sound a little boring to you, but it would BE a TON more boring if you were actually there. Not a single soul (appliance) in the store was happy.

No one ever came to buy a single headphone set, laptop, tablet, iPhone, microwave or fridge, because everybody in the whole world had already bought a TV set and their eyes were glued to it. They were all too lazy to come to the store.

The appliances were sitting, bored, on their dusty shelves. Even Pen Drive, the tiny but strong Super Gadget of the store didn't have anybody to save.

Fridge remarked, "Pen Drive, I think there could be something for you to do."

Pen Drive asked, "Well, why don't you tell me exactly what it is? I'm really bored!"

Everybody yelled, "WE ALL ARE!"

Fridge slyly said, "With all these people glued to that IDIOT BOX, there is an immense problem at hand. Even all the shopkeepers have gone to watch TV! Why don't we unglue the people from the set, or break it, to free the people?"

Pen Drive thought for a moment, then cried, "YES! It might just work! Let's ALL go!!!" And so, all of the gadgets stealthily sneaked out of the store to the people's houses!

When people saw walking, talking gadgets in their houses, they screamed and immediately turned the TV off to go and hide! And the neighbourhood was full of them!

The fridge apologized to all the gadgets as they ran, "Sorry the plan went wrong. But, look at the bright side! At least the people are unglued!"

And it was true! The people were not watching TV anymore! In fact, they were running out of their houses… Straight at the gadgets!

The gadgets ran away at lighting speed when they saw the people! When the people complained to the mayor, the mayor said it was all a hallucination. And the people believed him!

The gadgets never forgot this incident! They were glad that they had a great adventure, instead of wasting the day sitting on dusty shelves!

PEN DRIVE — THE SUPER GADGET

THE MAGIC BOOK

Having read the title, what do you think this story is about?

Do you think it is about a book of magic? Or if the book could sing, dance or fly unlike a normal book?

Well, not really! Before you cook up more thoughts on what this magic book could be about... Let me tell you what it actually IS.

This story is about a book, so marvellous and unique that readers get absorbed into it and talk and play with the characters in it!

Read more to unleash the amazing secrets of the book! Enjoy reading!

In a small town in Europe, lives an ordinary girl named Seena. She lives in a big bungalow with her pet parrot, Kana.

Seena loves to read. She has three full cupboards stacked with many books—big books, small books, tiny books, humungous books, heavy books and light books.

One morning, Seena heard the doorbell ring. When she opened the door, there was no one standing there. Kana saw a small package lying near the door. Seena noticed it too and picked it up. The package had her name on it! She decided to open it, and laid it out on the table. She tore the package slowly with her pen knife, and opened it.

FLASH!

A light flashed through the room. Seena could see the light was coming from a book, which was inside the package. Seena opened the book.

POOF!

Seena had disappeared with Kana! She didn't know what was happening. She was twirling around, in a tornado, with stars and planets circling around her!

FLASH!

The light flashed once again. Everything around her turned white. She noticed that there were words written above her head. Seena suddenly felt her pocket turn heavy. She found a pack of crayons in her pocket. She looked up and read the words, "There was once a very funny and cheerful clown."

A thought suddenly struck her mind, "It seems I am in a book. Look! The page ends there! I can go over there, lift the page and do the same for all the rest of the pages until I get out of the book!"

Yes! Seena loved books so much that she got IN a book.

And so, she ran to the end of the page and tried to lift it in vain. She exclaimed, "Oh no! The page is too heavy! I cannot lift it! But wait! Why is a pack of colourful crayons in my pocket? And why is there a sentence above my head?"

She took a red crayon and drew a red ball, on the white page. Then— "Oh look! The page is turning! Let me complete the clown!"

As the ball looked like a red nose, and the page slightly shook, Seena understood that if she illustrated every sentence of the book, she could get out of it! She told Kana, "Come on, Kana, help me draw! Let's get out of here!"

After they completed drawing the clown, and were about to go to the next page, the clown suddenly yelled, "I'll come too! Take me with you!" Seena was surprised to hear the clown speak. She agreed, and the clown cheerfully hopped along.

"My name is Roger", said the clown, "And I have lived in this book for a long time, waiting for someone to draw me and give me company! Thank you for freeing me!"

Seena introduced herself, "I am Seena, and this is my pet parrot, Kana. We have come here by accident, because this morning…".

"Oh, is it morning?", interrupted the clown. "I haven't come alive in a long time! I don't know what time it is, or anything else."

Seena continued, "Now it must be Saturday afternoon. This morning, I received a package with my name on it, and inside it was this book…" She narrated the whole story.

The clown said, "I have explored this book many times. It has a lot of pages. I know a way we can get out, without having to flip those pages. Draw a man holding a wand and wearing a hat and a cloak. The picture will become a wizard, and he will magic us out of here." Seena drew as he told, and soon, a friendly wizard appeared. He waved his wand— ZAP!

The trio disappeared from the book and reappeared safely back home. Seena asked Roger if they could be friends, and he could live with them.

The clown said, "This book is my home. Although I haven't been outside in a long time, I'm afraid I cannot stay here with you. Do keep this book with you, though. Whenever you open the book, you can visit me! And I will visit you regularly too!"

The two new friends bid each other goodbye, and as the clown opened the book— FLASH!!!

He had disappeared again!

Seena told Kana, "That was an excellent adventure, right? And we made a new friend!" Kana tweeted joyously. None of them ever forgot this magical incident!

Tanmayishri Sumanth

SEENA'S NEW FRIEND

THE BIG PROBLEM

Dear reader,

As you may have seen in the introduction poem — 'What is this book about?', I have mentioned that ALMOST all the stories in this book are fictional.

This particular one is a mixture of fiction and non-fiction.

But nothing in this story has happened in real life, in case you get any doubts!

The gods had had enough. Almost every mortal on earth was complaining about not having enough day, or that the night was too short. The gods just didn't know what to do. But, if they didn't do something, the cranky mortals would give them many more sleepless nights.

Finally, Lord Indra, the king of the gods, decided to mix the moon and sun together, so the mortals would get an equal amount of day and night (like a mother who stops her children fighting for a cookie by breaking it in two halves). And that's how Surya (the sun god) and Chandra (the moon god) ended up in Indra's palace to get mixed.

Surya was yellow, and Chandra was blue. They looked rather uncomfortable. They didn't want to be mixed. After a few hours, Indra had thoroughly mixed them. The sun and moon did NOT exist anymore! There was only—

THE SMOON

The Smoon (sun + moon) was sent to space to be orbited around by the planets. The moon couldn't orbit around earth, as a part of it was attached to the large, hot sun. The whole universe (all the humans, animals, even aliens!) didn't like the new sun and moon.

The life forms on earth began to have a lot of trouble with the Smoon. People didn't know when to sleep, because the sky was always divided into two parts—the Reddish Yellow part and the Dark Blue part.

All the clocks stopped ticking, the watches stopped working, the cock stopped crowing, and the alarms stopped beeping. Every way of telling time had stopped abruptly! Now everyone was confused. People, animals and plants started dying, due to limited sunlight and sleep.

After the Smoon turned up in the sky, even the water cycle stopped, because there wasn't enough sunlight! Neither the process of evaporation nor that of condensation could take place. Thus, there was lack of water, and all the living beings suffered.

People started to request the sages to create a path to the heavens, and to put an end to this. The gods realized what was going on and informed this to Indra.

Indra, without hesitation, called the Smoon to his palace and separated them. After a second, the sun rose and it was morning, and eventually, twelve hours after that, came the moon at night.

The people were grateful that everything was back to normal, and they never raised a single complaint against the natural happenings.

So, it is a warning for all of us to—NEVER disregard nature, or think that it can be improved.

Everything in this Universe is made the way it is, only for the good of mankind!

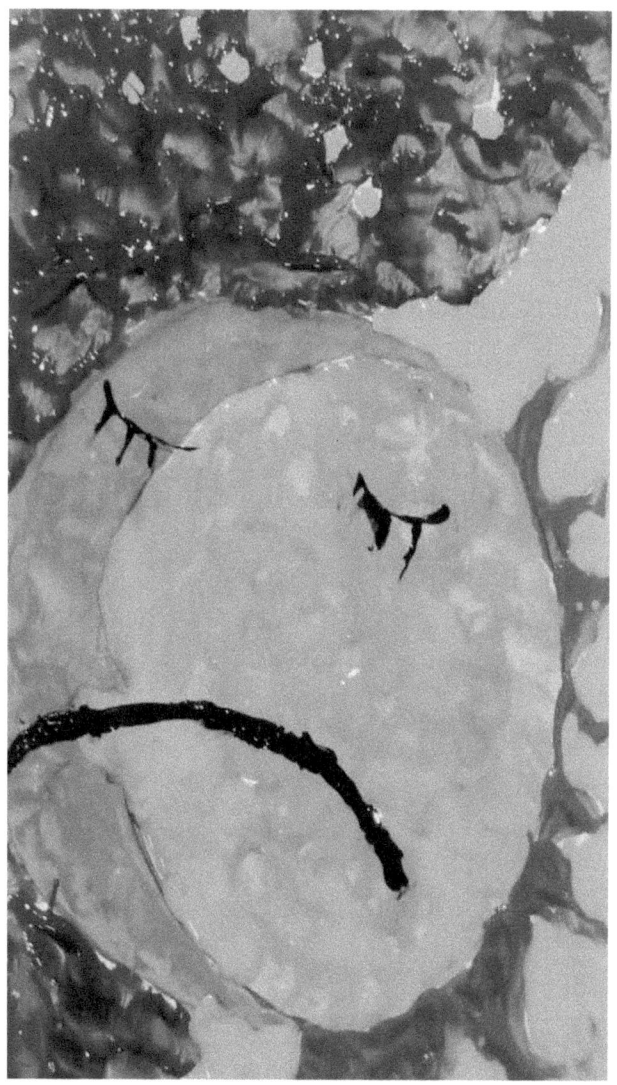

THE SMOON

MY DREAM LAND

This poem is made of things, characters and occurrences that are evidently impossible in real life. It is all only a figment of my imagination. Don't believe all that you read! Enjoy reading!

The land of topsy turvy things,
Full of crazy stuff!
Rocks and stones are really soft,
Cotton is quite rough!

Birds are neighing everywhere,
Look! A horse is chirping!
Hey! What is that artist using?
Using MUD, for painting!

Who will drive the plane?
It's a duck, of course!
Also, the fools are very sane,
And jokers feel morose!

Oh look! A thief robbed the bathroom!
He took away my toilet!
Call the police! What's his name?
It's Mr. Piglet!

Mr. Piglet saved the toilet!
How can I repay him?
Ah! Of course! A mud bath!
I'll borrow some from Artist Rahim!

And, in this confusing place,
Let me conclude now,
The school teachers are all bulls,
The headmaster's a cow!

Wow! Look up in the sky!
It's a shooting buffalo!
Make a wish really quick!
Do it fast! Now!

There are many clouds on the ground,
Lift them, just try!
They all stand still, like a rock,
'cept rocks are in the sky!

Oh! It is time to sleep.
I have made the bed.
My bed is made of rocks,
Rather comfortable for my head!

CLOUDS ON THE GROUND AND ROCKS IN THE SKY

www.ingramcontent.com/pod-product-compliance
Lightning Source LLC
LaVergne TN
LVHW061549070526
838199LV00077B/6974